He's the Prince of Pranks!

Knighty-Knight

FOR LOUIE POOLE,
WITH LOTS OF LOVE
S.M.

FOR MY LOVELY NEWBORN
NIECE, EVIE
M.B.

ORCHARD BOOKS
338 Euston Road, London NW1 3BH
Orchard Books Australia
Level 17/205 Kent St, Sydney, NSW 2000

First published in 2008 by Orchard Books
First paperback publication in 2009
Text © Sue Mongredien 2008
Illustrations © Mark Beech 2008

The rights of Sue Mongredien to be identified as the author
and Mark Beech to be identified as the illustrator of this work
have been asserted by them in accordance with
the Copyright, Designs and Patents Act, 1988.
A CIP catalogue record for this book is available from the British Library.

ISBN HB 978 1 40830 281 1
ISBN PB 978 1 84616 613 6

HB 1 3 5 7 9 10 8 6 4 2
PB 1 3 5 7 9 10 8 6 4 2
Printed in Great Britain
by CPI Cox & Wyman, Reading, RG1 8EX

Orchard Books is a division of Hachette Children's Books
an Hachette Livre UK company.
www.hachettelivre.co.uk

CHAPTER ONE

CRACK!

Prince Jake's cue ball smashed straight into the pack of red balls, sending them scattering all over the king-sized snooker table. It was a Thursday evening, and the Moranian royal family were in the games room, over in the east wing of their castle. "Yes!" Jake whooped, jumping up and punching the air as the white ball came to rest behind the brown.

"You are totally snookered, Dad!"

King Nicholas walked thoughtfully
around the snooker table, chalking his cue.
The Queen and Princess Petunia promptly
sprinted after him.

"I think you need to hit the cushion *here*,"
Queen Caroline said, pointing at a spot on
the side of the snooker table. "Then you can
pot *this* red ball."

"No, Mum," argued Princess Petunia,
who was Jake's big sister and thought she

6

knew everything. "If he gets the white to rebound from *here*, he can really stuff Jake for his next shot."

"Oi!" Jake cried indignantly. "Whose side are you on, anyway?"

"Don't worry, Jake," said Prince Ned, who was the youngest of the royal children, and currently playing pinball at the far end of the room. "Dad won't win. Dad never wins at anything."

"Hey, I heard that, you cheeky prince,"

7

the King grumbled. "That's no way to speak to a king, thank you very much!"

The King paced around the table once more, then crouched low over it, carefully positioning his snooker cue and closing one eye as he took aim. Jake blinked as his view of the table was suddenly obscured by his dad's rather large bottom. He had to really, REALLY resist the urge to give his dad a sharp prod with his own cue. It was so tempting...

But at that moment, there was a pattering sound...and then a whole chunk of the ceiling came loose, crashing right onto the middle of the snooker table with a mighty THUMP!

Jake blinked. Petunia squealed. And King Nicholas jumped, sending his cue skidding along the cloth and tearing it with a loud *rrrrriiiip*!

The cue ball went spinning across the table, bounced off the lump of plaster and rolled into a side pocket.

Jake grinned as plaster dust drifted down onto the King like snow. Talk about timing! "Oh dear!" he chortled, sliding his marker along five points on the scoreboard. "Unlucky, Dad!"

"This wretched castle!" fumed the King. His hair was white with dust, and he looked much older suddenly, like a royal Father Christmas. He brushed the dust from his

hair and shoulders, and glared up at the ceiling, which now had an ugly-looking hole in it. "One of these days, the whole place is going to collapse on our heads, you mark my words!"

"Well, the castle *is* one thousand years old, dear," the Queen pointed out.

"I know, but..." The King brandished his snooker cue irritably. "Sometimes I wonder whether it's right that we, the royal family of Morania, should live in such a...dump. Whether we should move somewhere more befitting. Somewhere modern, you know, with all the bells and whistles."

"What do you want bells and whistles for?" Ned asked, looking puzzled. "Are you joining a band or something?"

The King ignored him. "Can't even play a game of snooker without bits of the place falling down around our ears!" he grumbled.

Jake brightened. "Are you admitting defeat, then?" he asked. "Does that mean I win?"

"Certainly not!" the King replied. "I'm sick of people thinking they can beat me at everything. I'm the King, you know. Doesn't that count for anything?" And he flung his snooker cue down on the table with a clatter, and stormed out of the room.

There was a shocked silence as the rest of the royal family watched him go. "I... I didn't mean to upset him," Jake said in surprise. "I only meant..."

The Queen picked the lump of ceiling-plaster off the snooker table and gazed after the King's retreating figure. "Don't worry," she said to Jake in a low voice. "He's got a bee in his bonnet, that's all, because Cosmo is coming to stay tomorrow. You know how he winds your father up."

Jake nodded, understanding at once. Cosmo was the King's cousin, and the most competitive person Jake had ever met. Whenever he came to visit the royal family, Cosmo would always show off about his new luxury apartments, his fabulous holidays and his high-flying career. According to the Queen, Cosmo and Nicholas had gone to the same school when they were boys, and it had always been Cosmo who'd beaten Nicholas at sports events and exams. Yep, that would get on your nerves all right,

Jake thought, feeling a rare burst of sympathy for his dad. No wonder he was in such a grump!

"Is Cosmo staying for the party?" Jake asked, hoping that the answer would be no.

"Yes," the Queen replied heavily. "But at least while there are so many other people around, we'll be able to avoid him. I mean—" She clapped a hand to her mouth, not meaning to have been so honest.

"It's all right, Mum," Petunia said. "None of us like him either. And we'll all enjoy the party, whether he's there or not."

"Too right," said Jake. He was really looking forward to Saturday night. The royal family were hosting a medieval gala evening, which sounded brilliant fun. There was going to be some real jousting, loads of games and side-shows, plus an enormous medieval banquet. Yum! Hundreds of people had been invited, and asked to come in fancy dress. "Hey, Mum, what's happening about our costumes anyway?" Jake asked.

The Queen turned to him. "Ahh, I meant to talk to you about that," she said. "I've ordered you one each. They should arrive tomorrow."

There was something shifty about her expression that made Jake suspicious.

"You did order the Black Knight costume I wanted, didn't you?" he asked.

The Queen hesitated. "Well, the thing is, dear, we felt that the Black Knight…"

She paused. "Well, it's not quite the thing for a young prince, is it? Considering what the Black Knight actually did, and everything."

"But the Black Knight is a legend!" Jake said, stung. "He was brilliant!"

"The Black Knight was cool," Ned agreed.

The Black Knight was one of the most exciting characters in Moranian history, from about five hundred years ago. He'd fought lots of battles, but was best known for all the cheeky tricks he'd played on the royal family.

The Queen sighed. "I know there are lots of great stories about the Black Knight," she said, "but most people know him for all the *awful* things he did. Like knocking your ancestor, King Albert, off his horse, into the royal lake! And tricking poor old Queen Veronica into eating one of the

corgis, pretending it was roast duck!
And..."

Jake was chuckling. "I love that one.
Eating the corgi! So funny!"

Petunia rolled her eyes. "I think it's
disgusting. Absolutely horrible!"

"But anyway," the Queen went on.
"Your father and I decided it would be
more appropriate for you to wear
something else. You know what the press
are like, dear, they'd have a field day if
you were dressed up as the Black Knight."

"So what *are* we all wearing?" Petunia
wanted to know.

17

"Well, your father's going to be the court jester, so let's hope he cheers up in time," the Queen began. "I'm going to be a milkmaid…"

Jake burst out laughing. "Please say Petunia's going to be one of your cows!" he snorted.

Princess Petunia made a lunge for him, but the Queen stepped between them.

"No, Petunia wanted to be a medieval damsel, which I think will be lovely. Ned, you're going to be a minstrel, with a lute."

"Loot? Am I going to be a burglar?" Ned asked, frowning in confusion.

"A lute is an old-fashioned instrument, you pea-brain," Jake said. "And a minstrel is an old-fashioned musician. What about me, Mum?"

"You're going to be…" His mum couldn't seem to look him in the eye all of a sudden. "Well, there wasn't an awful lot of choice, dear, so…" She fixed him with a fake smile. "So you're going to be a peasant," she finished.

A peasant? A peasant! Jake was not happy about that. Not happy at all! "Why do *I* have to be the peasant?" he cried. "Why can't I just be a knight, or something exciting?"

"Oh, don't take it personally, dear," the Queen said. "It's only a costume. I thought you'd find it funny! And they didn't have a lot else in your size."

Jake made a humphing noise and marched out of the room. What a cheek, expecting him, a prince, to wear a peasant costume! Well – he wouldn't do it. He just wouldn't!

Checking the coast was clear, Jake hurried to find a phone so that he could make a secret call to the costume hire shop. There was no way he was going to the party as a medieval peasant. No way on earth!

CHAPTER TWO

The next day was Friday, which meant lessons as usual for the three royal children, followed by a formal dinner in honour of their guest, Cosmo.

"Ahh, there you are," he said, as Jake, Ned and Petunia arrived in the dining hall that evening. "Petunia – looking as radiant as ever, my dear. And boys – I'm glad to see you've inherited your mother's athletic build, rather than turning out to

be porkers like your dad." He guffawed
and elbowed King Nicholas in the ribs.

"Only joking, Nick," he said. "I say,
what was it we all used to call you at
school, again? Prince Pudding, or
something, ha ha! Poor old Nick. Used to
get a bit of a teasing, your dad," he
added, turning back to Jake, Ned and
Petunia. "Oh, we would tease him rotten."

"Sit down, children," the Queen said, interrupting hurriedly.

Jake glanced at his dad, whose face was scarlet. The King also seemed to be gripping his cutlery tighter than was strictly necessary and making a rather alarming grinding noise with his teeth.

"So, Cosmo," the King said, after a deep breath. "How's business?"

"Booming, dear boy, booming! I'm probably ten times richer than you by now, ha ha!" Cosmo replied. "Just bought a new holiday home on a little island off the coast – well, actually, I bought the whole island while I was at it. Might as well, eh?" He cast a rather snooty eye over the walls of the dining room. The room was painted a warm red, but you could still see the patch on one wall where Jake had thrown a bowl of yogurt at his sister's head during a family argument. It had been painted over several times, but the stubborn yogurty stain still showed through. Cosmo's eyes lingered on the stain for a few seconds before giving the King a sorrowful smile. "And here *you* are, in this old castle, after all these years! Bet you wish you could jaunt around like me a bit more, don't you? I just up and go wherever I please. Great fun!"

"We really like it here," Jake said defensively, as the King's neck turned red and hot-looking.

"Ahh, you are sweet, dear boy, trying to make your old pa feel better," Cosmo replied. "You can tell me what you *really* think of it later, when he's not around, ha ha!"

"So, anyway," the Queen said quickly. "Do you have a costume lined up for tomorrow, Cosmo?"

"I should say so!" Cosmo said. "I'm

dressing up as the King – not Nick, of course, I don't want to frighten any children, ha ha! No, I'm dressing up as the medieval King – King Wilhelm." He swigged from his goblet of wine and smacked his lips together. "It'll be a treat for all the guests to see a good-looking king like me swanning around the grounds for a change, eh? Ha ha!"

"They're used to seeing a good-looking king," Petunia told him curtly. "Daddy. Your host. Remember?"

Jake saw the Queen give his sister a warning glance. "That's enough, Petunia," she said.

"Well, he's being really rude about Dad, and—"

"That's *enough*," the Queen repeated. "Ahh, good, here comes the food."

It was rare that Jake agreed with his sister about *anything*, but he couldn't help a sneaking feeling of respect for her now, sticking up for their dad like that. Cosmo was so awful! No wonder Jake's mum and dad had been dreading him coming here.

Silence fell for a moment as Boris, the royal butler, and Mrs Pinny, the housekeeper, brought in silver trays of food. "We have smoked salmon, quails' eggs, caviar..." Mrs Pinny began, reeling off the extensive list of goodies the kitchen staff had prepared.

Jake brightened as he saw a plate of fat sausages and a plump roast chicken arrive on the table. Mrs Pinny even plonked down a dish of Jake's favourite

26

fluffy mashed potato in front of him. "'Specially for you, Your Highness, just the way you like it best," she said with a curtsey.

"Mmmm, thanks!" Jake said, licking his lips.

Cosmo, on the other hand, didn't look impressed. "Chef having a night off, eh?" he said dismissively, turning his nose up at the steaming platters Boris was setting down. "Oh dear. I'm not that hungry, actually. I might just phone out for a takeaway later."

The King dazzled Mrs Pinny and Boris with a smile. "This looks wonderful," he told them. "Thank you very much. We're all very grateful, I'm sure." And he poured himself another goblet of wine and drank it in one big gulp.

The meal began in uncomfortable silence. Jake was starting to feel really sorry for his dad, and annoyed with Cosmo. What a cheek – him coming to stay with them, and having nothing but rude things to say!

The Queen was still trying her best to be a good hostess. "So, did Nicholas tell you much about tomorrow's party, Cosmo?" she asked. "We're having a medieval banquet in the great hall, and we're going to light up the grounds of the castle with floodlights, so that we can have a jousting event outside, and..."

"What's jousting?" Ned wanted to know.

"It's what they used to do in the olden days," Jake explained. "Two knights would each have a horse and a lance – like a great long pole. And they'd ride towards each other and try to knock each other off their horses with the lances. Something like that, anyway. Sounds dead exciting."

"Jousting, eh?" Cosmo said, looking interested. "That should be fun. Can anyone take part?"

"Oh yes, of course," the Queen replied. "The more the merrier!"

"Good-o!" boomed Cosmo. "Well, you can count me in, then. Always was good at sports, wasn't I, Nick? School captain of the polo team, remember? Champion cross-country runner!"

Jake had had enough of Cosmo's boasting. "Well, Dad's good at loads of stuff, too," he said, although secretly he was having trouble thinking of anything. Did being good at eating count? "And I bet he'd be brilliant at jousting!"

The King gave him a tight smile. "Well, I'm not sure about that, Jake, but thanks for the support," he said. "I—"

"Oh, we should have a little contest, then!" Cosmo interrupted smoothly. "I'll take you on, Nick. That will be fun, won't it?"

Jake gazed at the King, feeling worried. He wished he'd kept his mouth shut now. As much as he loved his dad, Jake was sure that in any sort of sporting competition the King had with Cosmo, there would only be one winner. And it wouldn't be King Nicholas.

"*I* could joust with you, Cosmo," Jake suggested, hoping to save his dad from the embarrassment. "I'm pretty good on horseback."

Petunia let out a snort. "Good on horseback? Jake, you barely know one end of a horse from the other!" she cried. "If anyone's going to take on Cosmo, it should be me or Mum. We're both excellent horsewomen!"

Cosmo's lip was curling in a smirk.

"Sweet," he drawled. "All your family are vying to take me on, it seems, Nick. But not you! How amusing."

King Nicholas banged his wine goblet down on the table. "Of course I'll take you on," he declared. "And I'll joust you out of town, Cosmo!"

Jake felt alarmed at this fighting talk. What was his dad *saying*?

The Queen seemed rather anxious too. "It's only meant to be a bit of fun, remember, dear," she said, putting a hand on her husband's.

Cosmo's smile had stretched even wider. "Oh good," he replied to the King. "I *am* glad to hear you're game, Nick. How about making a little bet, so things are even more fun?"

"Anything!" the King replied, sloshing more wine into his goblet.

He was drunk, Jake realised in dismay. Oh, no! This was sure to lead to trouble.

"How about..." Cosmo leaned forwards, twiddling his moustache. "How about, if you win, I'll give you my new holiday home. Hey, I'll throw in the whole island, how about that?"

"Sounds good to me," the King replied.

"And if *I* win," Cosmo went on, "you give me this castle."

"What?" Jake cried. "You can't say that! This is our home!"

"Nick," the Queen said, turning to him with a nervous light in her eyes. "Don't

33

say anything you might regret..."

But the King was already stretching his arm across the table and shaking Cosmo's hand. "Done," he slurred. "It's a deal."

Jake, Petunia, Ned and the Queen all stared at each other in horror. "We are *so* going to be homeless!" Petunia hissed.

CHAPTER THREE

The next day was Saturday, and everyone
in the castle was busy putting the finishing
touches to all the preparations for the
evening's party. A spit was being built in
the fireplace of the great hall, to roast
a hog for the banquet. Boris was
welcoming the band and showing them
to the royal rehearsal room. Mrs Pinny
was cleaning the old wooden stocks
that were being used in a sideshow.

And Mr Chevalier, the royal groomsman, was brushing down the horses ready for the jousting contest.

While Cosmo went off for a walk around the grounds – no doubt planning what he'd do with them when he'd won the castle, Jake thought glumly – the rest of the royal family rallied around the King, who was now feeling very guilty about his drunken bet.

"You've got to win this, Daddy," Petunia told him, leading him towards the stables.

"We'll be the laughing stock of the whole world if we – the royal family! – are turfed out of our own home."

"Cosmo would never really do that," the King argued, but he didn't sound very sure.

"I bet he would," Jake replied. "He'd chuck us out like a shot! He can't wait to get his hands on this place."

"I heard him on his phone, telling someone he wanted to turn it into a theme park," the Queen said unhappily. "Surely he wouldn't be so heartless?"

"A theme park! Cool!" Ned said, his eyes lighting up at the thought. "Why didn't we think of that?"

"Well, let's not dwell on it now," the Queen said, flashing Ned a warning look. "Let's just get your father well and truly prepared for the jousting tonight. He's *got* to win!"

The King groaned and passed a hand over his head. "Stop saying that," he said. "You're making me feel really under pressure."

"Well, you *are* under pressure," Jake reminded him. "You're fighting to save our home, Dad."

"And you're the one who put yourself in this position," the Queen pointed out tartly, "so it's a bit late to be talking about pressure!"

The five of them had reached the stables now, and the Queen handed the King a riding hat from the tack room. "Put that on," she said. "I'll get you a horse."

Jake was no horse expert but even he could see that the King was a very nervous rider. After a full hour of coaching, his dad could do little more than stay upright on the back of Jessie, the most sweet-natured horse from the stables, while she was walking. If Jessie so much as went into a trot, the King turned white and clutched the reins with such terror in his eyes, it was as if he were riding on the back of a man-eating shark, Jake thought with a groan.

"Bang goes our castle," he said gloomily to Petunia as they watched the King fall off Jessie straight into a patch of thistles. "We are definitely going to be homeless by the end of the day!"

Petunia sighed heavily in agreement. "We're just going to have to really hope that Cosmo is even worse on horseback," she said.

They watched as the King scrambled to
his feet, tried to mount Jessie, and went
flying straight over her back, landing
this time in a huge mound of horse poo.

"Somehow I doubt it," said Jake.

After lunch, Jake was about to go and take a sneaky peek at some of the party preparations outside with Ned, when Alex, one of the junior butlers, beckoned him over. "A special delivery for Your Royal Highness has just arrived," he said. "I've had it sent up to your bedroom, Prince Jake. Just in case it was a...secret."

Jake's eyes widened at Alex's words. "Thanks," he said. He turned back to his brother. "Ned, I've just got to do something," he yelled, dashing towards the sleeping quarters. "I won't be long."

Jake ran upstairs to his bedroom as fast as possible. If he wasn't very much mistaken, Alex was talking about his costume for the party. Not the peasant costume his mum had ordered for him, which looked as if it had been stitched out of a brown sack. Oh, no. With a bit of luck, the delivery might just be the

41

Black Knight costume Jake had ordered
from the hire shop!

Jake pushed open his bedroom door
and peeped inside. A grin spread across
his face as he saw what was lying on
his bed.

A black helmet with visor.

A black chestplate.

A black chainmail top.

And black armour for his legs.

Oh yes. Fantastic! He was going to look so cool as the Black Knight!

He put the helmet over his head and lifted the visor to peer out at his reflection in the mirror. It was a bit big, and the visor did keep slipping down with a rattle, but other than that, he looked sensational.

"Peasant indeed!" he scoffed to himself as he pulled on the rest of the armour and strolled around the room, loving the way he clanked with each footstep. He'd show his mum what *proper* fancy dress looked like!

Still grinning, he took the armour off again, stowed it carefully in his wardrobe where his mum wouldn't notice it, and went off to find Ned. The Queen had said that there would be hundreds of people coming to the party, hadn't she? She'd never notice if Jake sneaked off and became the Black Knight for part of it.

Jake slid down the long, curving banister, and an interesting thought struck him. Hey! Of course! If he was in disguise as the Black Knight, he might even be able to do something to stop Cosmo beating his dad at the jousting!

CHAPTER FOUR

At five o'clock that evening, the castle
gates opened, and the guests began
streaming in. Jake and Ned watched them
from the top tower of the castle. Some
people arrived by helicopter or private jet.
Others came in swanky cars. Everyone
was smiling and looking excited in their
fancy-dress costumes.

"Look, there's Cosmo," Jake said,
pointing down to the courtyard below

where Cosmo was greeting guests with his usual oily smirk. "Ugh, just watch him, he's acting as if he owns this place already!"

"We can't let him win our castle," Ned said fiercely. "Can't we lock him in the dungeon or something, until the jousting's over?"

Jake had been racking his brain about the jousting problem ever since he'd seen his Black Knight costume, but still hadn't come up with a brilliant plan of action. "We've got to do *something*," he agreed. "There's no way Dad will win the contest otherwise."

Boris appeared behind them just then. "Boys? Your mother's asked me to make sure you're putting on your costumes for the party," he said. "The banquet is due to begin in ten minutes, and then it'll be time for the jousting!"

Jake and Ned looked at each other in dismay. Ten minutes – was that all? They'd have to get a move on. Operation Nobble Cosmo had to get underway as soon as possible!

Ten minutes later, Jake and Ned joined the throng of guests as they all made their way into the Great Hall to eat. Jake was wearing his peasant costume for the time being, as he knew he'd have to sit near his parents for the meal. He certainly didn't want to give away the fact that he had a *second* fancy-dress outfit lined up. Not yet, anyway.

Wooden tables and benches had been set out in the Great Hall, and the King and Queen were already seated at the top table with Petunia. Jake and Ned slid into their places as the band of minstrels tuned up and then launched into their first song, "Glory of Morania".

There was a rousing burst of applause as the last notes of the chorus died away, and then the King stood up, and silence fell.

"Good evening, ladies and gentlemen!" he boomed, in his heartiest voice. "And welcome to the royal castle of Morania. We are delighted and honoured to have

48

you with us tonight, for our medieval gala evening. In a few moments, our chefs will be serving a medieval feast, and then we will proceed to the evening's entertainment. This will include dancing and merry-making, enjoying some old-fashioned stalls and sideshows in the castle grounds and, oh yes…" He coughed out the last word as if he didn't really want to say it. "Jousting."

There was a round of applause as the
King sat down, and then, to Jake's dismay,
Cosmo immediately jumped to his feet
and addressed the room. "Good evening,
ladies and gentlemen," he said. "I won't
keep you from your food for very long,
I promise. I just thought you'd like to
know about our very special attraction
tonight, which is that the King and I will
be jousting with one another! I hope
you'll all come and watch us a little later."
He grinned. "May the best man win, eh,
Your Highness?"

The band broke into a round of "For He's a Jolly Good Fellow", and there was more clapping. Then the servants began bringing out huge platters of food – a whole roast pig with an apple in its mouth, dishes of roast potatoes and vegetables, steaming gravy and crusty bread rolls – and everyone started tucking in.

Jake could hardly bring himself to eat, he felt so nervous about the jousting. How he wished Cosmo hadn't opened his big mouth and announced it to everybody! Now there was sure to be a huge crowd to watch the King being humiliated. And everyone would witness the royal family losing their beloved castle!

The King, too, was looking rather pale and sweaty, Jake noticed. And he was barely touching his food, which was an incredibly rare sight. He didn't even have extra helpings of roast potatoes! This was serious.

Cosmo had to be stopped!

As soon as the meal was over, Jake slipped away and up to his bedroom, where he put on his Black Knight costume once more. A plan was forming in his head. If he could somehow sneak a horse from the stables and gallop up to the jousting area, perhaps he could challenge Cosmo to joust with *him*, the mysterious Black Knight, instead of the King. Or maybe Jake could challenge the King himself – and let his dad win, to make him look less awful...

He had no time to lose, anyway. He had to get on a horse, and get over there, fast, before Cosmo ruined everything!

The stableyard was thankfully deserted when Jake arrived. Many of the horses were being used for the jousting event but luckily Jessie was still dozing in her stable.

"Come on, girl," Jake said softly, as he patted her to wake her up. "Don't be fooled by this armour. It's me, Jake. The Queen's son, yeah? So...d'you fancy an evening ride?"

Jessie harrumphed and gave a little whinny, which Jake took to mean yes.

Well, that was a good start, anyway. He strapped a saddle on her and carefully clambered on her back. "Now, Jessie," he said, stroking her dark mane. "I need a big favour. Me and you have somehow got to keep this castle in the hands of the royal family. Think you can help?"

Jessie whinnied again, a little louder this time.

"I was hoping you'd say that," Jake said, patting her neck. "Good girl. Let's go!"

Jessie had just started trotting off when Jake realised he'd forgotten to put a bridle and reins on her. "Oh – hang on a minute, Jessie," he said, but she didn't seem to understand. She carried on, her hooves making a soft clopping sound as she went.

"Whoa!" Jake said, louder this time, as he clung to the saddle and gripped her back with his knees. "Jessie...wait!"

CHAPTER FIVE

Jessie didn't want to wait. She didn't want to *whoa*. She just went on trotting out of the stableyard and down the track – in completely the wrong direction.

"Jessie!" Jake moaned in despair, as she clip-clopped through the dusk towards the royal lake. "You're going the wrong way!" He groaned, wishing that horses came with steering wheels on their heads, so you could at least get them to take you where

you wanted to go. How *did* you steer
a horse, anyway? He tried digging his
knees in a bit tighter, but that only made
Jessie break into a gallop. And then the
visor came clunking down on his helmet
and Jake could no longer see where they
were going!

"Whoa-oa-oa!" he cried helplessly.
"Sto-o-o-op!"

Jake clung on for dear life as Jessie
bounced him along the track. By
crouching low over her neck, he managed
to push up his visor with one hand while
holding on tightly around Jessie's neck
with the other. "Jessie," he croaked, trying
to sound as calm and soothing as he
could manage. "Please, Jessie, please...just
slow down a bit, will you?"

Jessie didn't seem to understand "slow
down", but she at least took the hint that
Jake wasn't enjoying the ride. Just as he

was starting to fear they'd be galloping all
night long, she proceeded to stop dead,
sending Jake soaring off her back and into
a muddy puddle.

SQUELCH! CLANG!

Bits of his armour clashed together and
dug into his skin as he landed. Ouch!

Mud sprayed everywhere, some ending
up in his eyes and mouth. Ugh!

Jessie bent her head and began cropping the grass at the side of the track, as if Jake wasn't even there.

Jake got to his feet with difficulty. Ouch. Why did horses have to be so high up, anyway?

"Jessie," he said, in his sternest voice. "Stop mucking about. We've got to get down to the jousting arena. We've got to help Dad – you know, the lardy idiot who was trying to ride you yesterday. He's in big trouble, Jessie. And it's down to us to sort him out!"

Jessie cocked an ear as if she were listening, then raised her head and turned towards Jake.

"Good girl," he said thankfully. "Come on."

Jake led Jessie back to the stable where he slung on a bridle and reins as best as he could. Then he climbed back into the saddle and made the clicking noise that he'd heard his mum make to the horses. "Come on, girl," he said. "Let's find the jousters, eh?"

This time, with a sharp tug on the reins, he managed to get Jessie trotting in the right direction. As evening fell it was getting darker by the minute, but Jake was guided by the bright floodlights of the jousting arena down the hill in front of him. He had no idea how long he'd been gone now – it seemed like ages!

For all he knew, the King and Cosmo may already have had their contest and the castle might very well be in Cosmo's hands now!

The thought was so terrible that Jake urged Jessie on and she broke into a gallop. "Nearly there," he panted, as she scudded across the royal lawn. "Please let us still be in time!"

They were approaching the area where the jousting arena had been set up. Huge lights had been hung from the castle walls, so that this particular part of the grounds was as brightly lit as if it were full daylight. And what a sight it was, too! Flags of all colours waved in the wind. Medieval-style marquee tents had been set up, and Jake could see a juggler and a fire-eater entertaining the crowds of people who'd gathered. It looked brilliant!

Ahh – and there was the jousting section itself, with a long red dividing rail down the centre, and horses in their medieval tack lined up at either end. They looked rather as if they were wearing colourful dresses and hoods, Jake thought to himself.

There was no sign of his father anywhere. Jessie slowed as they drew up on the edges of the crowd, and Jake patted her as she stood there, breath streaming from her nostrils in the cool evening air. "Wait here a moment," Jake whispered in her ear. "Let's just see if we can spot Dad and Cosmo."

At that moment, Jake saw a herald, who was carrying the royal family's coat of arms on a banner, step up to the front of the crowd. "My lords, ladies and gentlemen!" he cried.

Silence fell, and the fire-eater and juggler bowed quickly and moved out of the way.

"I am proud to announce that our jousting event is about to begin," the herald went on. "And as you heard earlier, the King himself is going to take part!"

Polite applause broke out amongst the

crowd, but Jake just felt a lurch inside at
the words. This was all his fault. If he'd
kept quiet at the dinner table the other
day, this wouldn't be happening!

"I gather from the King's cousin, the
honourable Cosmo Worthmore, that there
is an interesting bet riding on the outcome
of their joust," the herald went on. "Ladies
and gentleman, our noble King is so
confident of his superior jousting skills,
he has bet his castle on it!"

The crowd gasped at this news, and Jake groaned. So now everyone knew about his dad's stupid bet! This got worse and worse. Everyone would see the King's humiliating defeat – and everyone would see the royal family made homeless. What a total disaster!

He gripped Jessie's reins, and took a deep breath. He was going to have to act soon if he was to prevent this joust from going ahead. "So what I'll do, is..." he muttered to himself. Then he stopped. What *was* he going to do, anyway? He'd never actually worked out the finer details.

"So now I beg of you, my lords and ladies, to be upstanding for King Nicholas the Second of Morania, and his jousting rival, Mr Cosmo Worthmore!" cried the herald.

Trumpets blasted in a royal fanfare, and there were rousing cheers and applause from the crowd, as they all scrambled to their feet. Then in rode two horses, one on each side of the dividing rail. One horse was dressed in red-and-black checked tack, the other in blue and gold.

Cosmo was on the left side of the rail, riding the red and black horse with ease and grace. He flourished his red lance in the air and smiled at the crowd as his horse trotted along, its head proudly up. Cosmo had full armour on, just like a medieval knight, with a red feathery plume flowing from his helmet.

Jake gulped. Suddenly he didn't feel quite so confident about galloping down there and taking on his uncle. Cosmo looked pretty formidable in his jousting get-up. One whack from that lance of his, and Jake would be on the floor.

He looked anxiously at the rider on the second horse, which was further back. His dad had somehow squeezed himself into what looked like a too-small set of armour, but his visor was down – probably so that the crowd couldn't see just how nervous he was, Jake guessed. Still, at least the King was managing to wave the blue lance in the air as his horse trotted along to loud cheers from the crowd, which was something. And he hadn't actually fallen off the horse yet, so that was better than yesterday...

There was another trumpet fanfare, and then the herald stepped up once more.

"Your Majesty, Cosmo…if you could go to your starting places now, please?" he asked politely. "Ladies and gentlemen, as you know, the aim of the joust is to break the opponent's lance – or even unseat them from their horse. At the sound of the trumpets, our contestants will ride towards one another and do battle. Please be silent as they prepare."

Jake watched with mounting despair as the King trotted to the far end of the jousting run, and Cosmo came to the end nearest Jake. He couldn't believe this was actually about to happen! He had to do something – and fast!

Both horses turned to face one another.
Then the trumpet players raised their
trumpets to their lips, and blew a fanfare,
and the jousting horses both began running.
It was starting!

Jake dug his heels into Jessie's side and
galloped towards them, his heart pounding.
"Wait!" he cried frantically. "Stop!"

CHAPTER SIX

The crowds scattered to either side of Jake and Jessie as they thundered down to the jousting run. "It's the Black Knight!" he heard people saying in surprise. "What's happening?"

Jake could hear the blood rushing in his head as Jessie galloped. He had to stop his dad and Cosmo before they met in the middle of the run! "I come to issue a challenge!" he roared through the slit in his helmet. "I—"

But whatever else Jake was going to say

was lost – as Jessie tripped on a thick tangle of electrical cables at the edge of the run, kicking them hard as she did so. She managed to keep her balance and continue running, but in the next second, the floodlights went out, as did all the electrics in the area. The entire jousting arena was plunged into darkness!

"Whoooooaaaa!" yelled Jake as Jessie went on galloping through the darkness.

CRASH! What was that they'd just bashed into?

CLANG! THUMP! "Ow!" came a muffled voice.

"Help!" came shouts from the crowd. "What's going on?"

Jake hadn't a clue where Jessie was taking him but she was still going. He could hear other horses neighing nervously in the darkness, and he pulled hard on Jessie's reins, trying to stop her before she knocked into anything else.

FLASH! Suddenly the floodlights came on again, dazzlingly bright now. Jake slipped off Jessie, lifted his visor and stared around. The King was in front of him, still on horseback, but not moving.

And behind them… *Ooops*, thought Jake.

Behind them, lying on the ground, his lance broken in two places, was Cosmo.

Right. So that thing Jessie had barged into must have been Cosmo's horse. And the thud Jake had heard must have been Cosmo falling off!

Princess Petunia rushed onto the jousting run just then with a scream of excitement. "Cosmo's down! That means Daddy's won!"

"Hooray!" cheered the crowd, all rising to their feet and applauding. They seemed to think the whole episode of the lights going out and back on again was part of the event.

The trumpeters broke into a second round of "For He's a Jolly Good Fellow", and the King punched the air in triumph, to more cheers.

"No!" Cosmo yelled. "That's not fair, I... Ouch!" He winced as he tried to stand up, and clutched his leg. "Get me an ambulance!" he wailed. "It hurts!"

The herald rushed back on, with a team of medics, who helped Cosmo onto a stretcher and took him away. "Ladies and gentlemen," the herald said, "our mighty King has triumphed...and has won the bet!"

"Hoooray!" cheered the crowd.

Re-sult! thought Jake. So much for the Black Knight causing trouble for the royal family – this time, the Black Knight had saved the royal family's necks!

"Thank goodness for that," muttered a voice near Jake's head.

He swung round in surprise, staring at

the armoured figure on horseback next to him. The armoured figure he'd assumed was the King. But the voice he'd just heard had sounded more like...

"Mum?" he asked in a low voice. "Is that *you* in there?"

A quiet chuckle came through the visor of the horse-rider's helmet. "Of course it is!" came his mum's whispered reply. "You didn't think I'd really put your father on horseback against Cosmo, did you? And have him lose our home? There was no way I was ever going to let *that* happen."

Jake laughed and laughed. "I did think that armour would be a bit tight on Dad," he said. "Nice one, Mum. What did you do with Dad?"

"He's up in the tower, watching the whole thing with a pair of binoculars," the Queen replied. Then her tone changed. "Where did you get that costume from, by the way? I thought I said no to the Black Knight?"

Jake hesitated, caught off guard. Luckily, Ned was running over, shouting something.

"Hey! I just thought! If Cosmo's lost the bet, does that mean we get his island?"

"This is your captain speaking," a voice said over the tannoy. "Please fasten your seatbelts. We are preparing to land."

Jake wriggled excitedly in his seat on the royal family's private jet. It was exactly two days after the medieval gala, and the

King and Queen had decided the whole family deserved a little holiday. Jake peered out of the aeroplane window. The sea sparkled turquoise below them, and he could just make out the sandy beaches and green mountains of an island in the distance. Ahh. That would be it. The royal family's new holiday island, thanks to Uncle Cosmo!

The Queen turned round from the seat in front of Jake and smiled at him. "I am *so* looking forward to this holiday," she said happily.

The King chortled. "Me too," he replied.

76

"Always said that Cosmo was a decent bloke."

"Daddy! You've never said that in your life!" Petunia protested, pushing her new diamond-studded sunglasses on top of her head in order to stare accusingly at him.

"He *did* give us his island, though," Ned put in, through a mouthful of toffees. "I might even send him a postcard."

"Or a get-well card," Jake said, still gazing out of the window. The jet was getting closer and closer to the island now, and he could see just how big the stretch of beach was, and how clear and warm the sea looked. There were boats moored to a jetty and – cool! – a whole line of jet-skis too. "Poor old Cosmo. Stuck in hospital with a broken ankle, while we're off on holiday..." He shook his head and grinned. "The party really did turn out to be a *black night* for him, didn't it?"

LOOK OUT FOR MORE
RIGHT ROYAL LAUGHS WITH

Sticky Gum Fun
978 1 84616 618 1   £3.99

It's Snow Joke!
978 1 84616 614 3   £3.99

Dungeon of Doom
978 1 84616 617 4   £3.99

Knighty-Knight
978 1 84616 613 6   £3.99

Monster Madness
978 1 84616 615 0   £3.99

Swordfights and Slimeballs!
978 1 84616 616 7   £3.99

Here's a taster of

Monster
Madness

"Pssst! Over here!"

Prince Jake jumped. He'd been rushing across the Great Hall with his brother and sister, on the way to breakfast, and the urgent whisper had taken him by surprise. "Who said that?" he asked, gazing around.

His brother, Prince Ned, pointed up at the stuffed head of a wild boar that hung on a wall nearby. It had bulging eyes, long sharp tusks and matted hair. "I think it was *him*," he said in alarm.

Jake rolled his eyes. "Don't be daft!" he said. "Stuffed animals don't—"

"Psssst! *Here!*" came the whisper again.

"It's definitely that warthog," Ned said nervously, stepping back.

Princess Petunia snorted, sounding very much like a wild boar herself. "For starters, it's a *boar*, not a warthog," she said. "And it's been dead about two hundred years by the looks of it."

PICK UP A COPY OF

Monster Madness
TO FIND OUT WHAT HAPPENS NEXT!

The *Prince Jake* books are available from all good bookshops,
or can be ordered direct from the publisher:
Orchard Books, PO BOX 29, Douglas IM99 1BQ.
Credit card orders please telephone 01624 836000 or fax 01624 837033 or visit our
website: www.orchardbooks.co.uk or e-mail: bookshop@enterprise.net for details.
To order please quote title, author and ISBN and your full name and address.
Cheques and postal orders should be made payable to 'Bookpost plc.'
Postage and packing is FREE within the UK
(overseas customers should add £2.00 per book).
Prices and availability are subject to change.